MAGICAL
FOOTSTEPS

By Anita Kirk

<u>Dedication</u>

Anita's most popular fan would be her father before he sadly got dementia, and he is now devastatingly blowing in the wind. Anita's family has supported her one hundred percent with her writing, and she thanks them for the encouragement and you for taking the time out of your day to pick her book up and read it.
If you do enjoy reading this book Anita would really appreciate a good review to show other people that you have enjoyed reading.

Acknowledgments

I would like to thank you for taking the time to pick this book out from the millions of books available out there to read, if you do enjoy reading this book, your review would mean the world to Anita Kirk for her to enjoy reading and sharing this book with others on social media or in person would be most appreciated.
Thank you.

Table of contents

Follow and message Anita Kirk any questions that you may have on Twitter, good reads, Linkedin and Facebook.

Written by Anita Kirk.

The places in this book are real.

Wakefield and Leeds are places in West Yorkshire, in the United Kingdom.

Scarborough is in North Yorkshire in the United Kingdom.

The Alpamare, the Diving Belle statue, Blackpool Pleasure Beach and the Sea Life Centre are real.

Blackpool is in the North west coast of the United Kingdom.

Prologue

Warning, this book will make you laugh so much with clean funny moments and jokes all the way from start to finish, get your tissues ready to wipe your tears of laughter away.

Ethan loses his friends Neil and John, with only their shoes left behind.

Ethan puts a spell on the shoes left behind with Witch Wakefield's help, Ethan then donates the shoes to the charity shop.

Arran and Jim purchase the shoes unknowingly that a spell was cast on them.

As they left the shop, Ethan knocked Neil and John out with the Geek flower and then later informed them that Arran would be travelling to Blackpool to find John and Jim, and they would also travel to Scarborough to find Neil.

Jim finds trouble in Blackpool, and Arran ends up at the Savoy Hotel with less than a pleasant stay, and do Arran and Jess find John?

Does Jim find Neil while under attack?

They enter into a computer game that other people get a buzz out of watching things unfold from Scarborough to Blackpool and beyond.

Do they get their own back by putting the evil people into the unpredictable game?

You need to read to find out.

Get ready for an enjoyable clean adventure for all ages to enjoy that all eyes will be glued to all over the globe by many book lovers out there of all ages.

Magical footsteps

Chapter One

Broken

"Hello, my name is Arran, I am twenty-five and I live in Leeds in the United Kingdom alone, my shoe heel has just broken, there are no shoe shops nearby so I am just going into this charity shop to find a pair of shoes that fit me perfectly, I have tried these shoes on, and they fit me superbly, I will buy these plain black leather shoes please!"

The old lady volunteer behind the till said as he was paying. "Use them wisely!"

The tall, slim-built male customer behind him bought a similar pair of black shoes, with the short lady volunteer at the till saying. "Use them wisely!"

Arran was about to walk outside wearing the shoes with his old shoes in a carrier bag with the man behind him speaking to Arran. "That's strange because she said the same thing to me, my friend used to eat fortune cookies with the fortune inside, people say that he chews wisely."

The man who was standing behind Arran smiled, replying. "Yes, it was a little bit strange her saying that to us both, it is nice to meet you my name is Jim and your appetite for friends is a little bit odd with him eating the whole fortune cookie, and your amazing choice in future friends makes your life better if you don't mind me saying and I feel like we are being watched, and we look about the same age!"

Arran guessed, looking a little puzzled. "If you are twenty-five, then yes you are the same age as me, I take it that you are hinting that you want to be my friend, it is turning out to be a strange day isn't it Jim, and yes life can be a little bit odd sometimes!"

Jim sounded surprised. "I am the same age as you, which is strangely unusual and yes, it is nice to have many friends, and I noticed a strange man looking at us hanging around near to the outside door of the charity shop earlier with him looking unusually strange at us!"

Arran felt uneasy. "Look, that man is staring at us again, I think that's so rude!"

Jim spoke loudly so that he could hear. "Please just ignore him, he must be a weirdo, or he has got nothing better to do!"

Arran looked at the stranger staring at them. "Look, it is even more unusual because he is looking down at our shoes and smiling like he is plotting something for us!"

Arran and Jim walked outside with a tractor in the car park as they walked out of the door with people staring at it, gossiping with them all saying. "I wonder what the lady serving behind the counter means by using the shoes wisely?"

Suddenly, Arran and Jim, who had bought the shoes, got scooped up into a tractor's grippers, with them dropping into the bottom of the trailer, taking them away with it blowing smoke into their faces, slowly knocking them out, with them steadily going more drowsy. "Where is this clean-shaven male driver in this tractor taking us, and I feel injured from my body being bashed around?"

Arran passed out and then woke up with a man standing at the side of him with a silver key in his hand. "Hello, my name is Ethan, you have both been out cold for a day and you have been chosen, sorry about the uncomfortable journey here, I have patched your wounds up, it is the only way that I thought of to get you here and knocking you both out with the smell of the special yellow geek flower that I have invented, it has got sleeping powers in it when near to you, I activate it with this tiny key, I am glad that it did the ideal job that I needed it to do!"

"Hi, my name is Arran, what exactly are you saying, Ethan?"

Ethan demanded. "I need you both to help me, please!"

Arran asked. "How can me and Jim help you? I feel like getting the police involved right now because I feel so lightheaded with what you have done!"

Ethan pleaded. "You will both be okay, we need to find out what happened to the person who owned the shoes that you have just bought, everywhere that you walk, it will eventually take you to each place where the previous person went!"

Chapter Two

Witch Wakefield

Arran quizzed. "How does that work, Ethan, and why is the previous person who owned the shoes so important?"

Jim asked. "I am just trying to lighten the mood, does anyone else feel strange looking in the mirror?"

Arran replied. "Not really, no, maybe it's just me!"

Jim sounded surprised. "You gave the answer to my joke, how cool!"

Ethan looked serious. "I went to Witch Wakefield the other day to help me to put a spell on your shoes that you are both now wearing to take us hopefully back to my friends John and Neil who have gone missing with just their shoes left behind on my farm that you are both wearing!"

Arran mentioned. "We need to go to this Witch Wakefield to see if we can do anything else to find them, it sounds a bit like some sort of magical invisible tracking device!"

Jim agreed. "I also think that it is amazing with the spell on our shoes having a memory showing us the correct way to go, in my way of working it out, our shoes are some kind of magical satellite navigation system!"

Ethan explained. "Yes, it is clever, and the witch is called Witch Wakefield, and she lives in Crofton, Wakefield, let's go in my tractor, but this time you can squeeze on the seat next to me now that I know that you are both going to comply with me instead of being against me and you will hopefully help me to find John and Neil!"

Arran sounded flustered. "I am finding it hard to walk because the shoes are wanting to take me in the opposite direction!"

Ethan explained. "They will do, because they have got a spell on them that Witch Wakefield placed on your shoes to make you go everywhere, they will take you to every place that John went, Blackpool in the United Kingdom was John's favourite place with the happy-go-lucky feel!"

Jim looked confused. "My shoes are behaving in the same way, and do you know what witches put on bagels?"

Ethan asked. "I don't know, and your shoes may go to Scarborough in the United Kingdom a lot because that was Neil's favourite place!"

Jim answered. "Scream cheese is a witch's favourite food, and I take it that we just go where the shoes take us and inform you where we are?"

Ethan explained clearly. "Yes, you will know when you are close to John and Neil because Witch Wakefield says that the lampposts' lights will flash on and off, that is also part of her spell!"

Arran looked in deep thought. "That reminds me, the other day a police officer flashed for me to stop, but I didn't stop, and how do we know if it is a false alarm with it maybe just having a dodgy light?"

Ethan asked. "Why didn't you stop for the police and yes you will have some false alarms, but we will just have to deal with them as they arrive, this is my telephone number, please put it into your phones and ring me immediately if you find John and Neil, and I will be there as soon as I can!"

Arran explained. "Okay, and I didn't stop the car because my ex ran off with a copper, and I thought that he was frightened that he was trying to bring her back to me because I had just got rid of her!"

Jim laughed. "That's funny."

Ethan smiled, waving at Arran and Jim.

Arran and Jim set off walking in the opposite direction, with <u>Arran leaving on a bus and arriving in Blackpool.</u> "All I need to do now is find John!"

A lady appeared in front of Arran. "My name is Jess, and I am probably about the same age as you, I am twenty-five, who are you?"

"I am looking for someone called John who was wearing these shoes, and this place reminds me of a sandwich that walked into the bar, but they refused to serve him because they weren't serving food!"

Jess smiled. "I like that, you are hilarious, and you will never find John because there are too many people with them all mingling in the enormous crowds together here!"

<u>**Jim arrived in Scarborough, leaving the train.**</u> "I can tell that it's not my steady walking pace, and Neil, you must be here somewhere, is this your house that you are taking me to?"

Chapter Three

Bump

A lady shouted out of the window. "I can hear you talking to yourself, and if you are an illegal squatter that used to live in our house, please leave now!"

"No, my name is Jim, I am looking for Neil, who has been at this house before, do you know where he has gone?"

"I am sorry, but I have got no idea who this Neil is, now please leave before I have you unwillingly removed by the police!"

Jim looked up at the streetlights. "I have got a joke for you, why did two fours skip their dinner, and I am sorry, but I don't believe you because that streetlight flashing is a sign that Neil is most probably here!"

The lady explained. "There is no one with the name Neil here now, and please tell me, what is the answer?"

Jim answered. "Because they had already eight!"

The lady laughed. "I like that, this is my joke, a man is walking home alone late one foggy night when behind him he hears: Bump! BUMP! BUMP! Walking faster, he looks back and through the fog, he makes out the image of an upright casket banging its way down the middle of the street towards him!!

BUMP! BUMP! BUMP!

Terrified, the man begins to run towards his home with the casket bouncing quickly behind him.

FASTER! FASTER! BUMP! BUMP! BUMP!

He runs up to his door, fumbles with his keys, opens the door, rushes in, and slams and locks the door behind him in a major panic.

However, the casket crashes through his door with the lid of the casket clapping.

Clappity-BUMP! Clappity-BUMP! Clappity-BUMP!

On his heels, the terrified man runs.

Rushing upstairs to the bathroom, the man locks himself in.

His heart is pounding, his head is reeling, and his breath is coming in sobbing gasps.

With a loud CRASH, the casket breaks down the door.

Bumping and clapping towards him.

The man screams and reaches for something, anything, but all he can find is a bottle of cough syrup!

Desperate, he throws the cough syrup at the casket...

And...

The coffin stops.

Jim smiled. "That joke was so cool and better than mine, it cheered me up, I am sorry for interrupting you!"

"I am glad that you liked it, it was nice to meet you, and I am sorry, but I am now shutting the door now, bye!"

Back in Blackpool, Jess was speaking. "Arran, you look like a lost dog with you just wandering around like you don't know where to start, and how do you find your lost dog in the woods?"

Arran asked. "What is the answer Jess and there has got to be a sign of John somewhere, all I have got to do is keep on looking, my shoes have fetched us to the Savoy Hotel, I like the buzz and good atmosphere here in Blackpool!"

"Look up a tree and listen for the bark, and at least you can have a sit-down and something to eat with me, Arran, even if you don't find John!"

"That is comical, let's walk inside and enjoy some food and drinks and see if John is about because the food smells divine!"

"What is that banging noise, you wait there, Jess, while I investigate more!"

A restaurant male worker left the room where the knocking was and spoke to his colleague. "We need to stop him knocking on the cage door or our customers may get suspicious and go inside to investigate more!"

Arran sat back down with Jess, expressing his thoughts. "I have worked out that I am more than sure that I think that it is John making the banging noises, he must be trying to get our attention to save him because that banging noise sounds like someone is trying to get some attention from someone, I hope that Jim is having more luck than me in finding Neil!"

Jess sounded concerned. "Let's stay the night Arran so that we can spy on the staff and customers with every move that they make, you sit there and enjoy the comfy chair taking the weight off your feet Arran while I go and book us in for the night, we will work this mystery out!"

Chapter Four

Dodgy

Jess walked over to the reception area, looking at them curiously. "You all look very nervous that work here, like there is something dodgy happening here!"

The receptionist looked shifty, moving her eyeballs around erratically. "We are just very busy with too much on our plates to do, with not enough time to do it all with us being snowed under with work, I am pleased to tell you that you are booked in now for the night, and do you know when computers have overheated?"

Jess replied, looking at the receptionist playing with her hands nervously. "I don't know how you know when computers have overheated and thank you for booking us in!"

The receptionist replied while tapping her hand up and down on the desk. "Because they need to vent, and you are very welcome if you need us, we are just a phone call or a short walk away!"

Jess laughed and then sat back down with Arran. "I think that you are right, the receptionist lady looked very happy but dodgy, like she was trying to hide something by putting up a front!"

Arran expressed his feelings. "I really do think that John is behind that door, Jess!"

Jess suggested. "Let's go up to our room now that we have eaten for a lay-down and to think of our next move, Arran!"

As they walked past the door that had a banging noise on it. "The door is locked, I have just tried the handle, Jess."

"Let's go and sit in the bar instead and watch the staff open the door to see if we can run in when someone opens the door, Arran!"

A staff member put a key in the door while speaking on the phone to someone. "I am going to feed him and control the game now!"

Back in Scarborough, Jim was panicking. "I am still convinced that Neil must be in that house, but I don't know how I am going to get inside to find out!"

The lady from the house shouted out of the window. "I can still hear you talking to yourself, I am watching you to make sure that you leave because you are definitely not coming inside of my home, I mean it, I will phone the police!"

Jim picked the phone up. "Okay, I am going, Ethan, it is me, Jim, I think that Neil must be here in this house in front of me, what should I do now?"

Ethan sounded happy. "I will come over to Scarborough now Jim, you need to book yourself into Toulson Court guest house and wait for me to get there!"

Jim walked into Toulson Court guest house, speaking to the lady with a badge saying Angie behind the counter. "I will book myself in, I will then go for a lie down before my friend Ethan arrives, please let me know when he arrives by sending him up to knock on my door!"

Hours later, there was a knock at the door, with Jim answering. "Come on, let's go to that lady's house, Ethan and I always knock on the door instead of ringing the doorbell, I think that I deserve a Nobel prize!"

Ethan laughed. "You are funny!"

Back in Blackpool, Arran was ready to run at the door as the hotel key had opened it. "I have grabbed hold of the key out of his hand; Jess, please, help me because he is trying to grab the key back to go inside and lock us out!"

Jess screamed. "I am grabbing his fingers, Arran!"

The man from the hotel sounded bossy explaining. "I will kill you both if you don't leave me alone because I have got a real, true life computer game to help control people who are relying and waiting for me to put things in place for them to do that I am in charge of at the moment, I love making people do things that they don't want to do!"

Arran shook his head in disgust. "Stop speaking rubbish, you have lost the plot; I have got a tight hold of the key now Jess, we need to have a quick look around to see if there are any signs of John around here!"

Jess sounded panicked. "I can't see anything in this kitchen area Arran, that man is about to shoot us, and there is nowhere to hide!"

The man shouted. "Neither of you will get out of here alive!"

Arran cried. "I will come and save you somehow Jess, we need to make sure that John isn't there and stay alive!"

Jess scanned the kitchen with her eyes. "That silver tray is a good tool to use, and this sharp knife is good to protect us as a shield, Arran!"

Chapter Five

Terrified

Arran sniffled. "Yes, it is or knock them out with it, but the only problem is that it doesn't cover all of our bodies, because I have just been shot on my left foot with me leaving a trail of blood as I walk Jess, and he is reloading his gun to put us in more danger!"

Jess cried. "That gunshot was so deafeningly loud with it hardly smelling of anything, but it had a slight burning smell, I feel so scared for our lives, look, I have just found another tray that was on the side to protect us, Arran."

Arran demanded. "Edge towards the door with me so that we can leave, my left foot hurts so much, Jess."

Jess sounded concerned. "I will do; do you need help to walk Arran?"

Arran limped. "I could do with some help, let's just get out of here before we are both shot, Jess!"

Jess looked terrified with fright. "Grab my hands we are nearly out of here, oh wow I have just found a gun lying on the floor, it is your lucky day because you are going to be dead for shooting Arran, then we can steal your shoes for John to wear when we have eventually found him!"

The man screeched. "Please don't shoot me because I have got too much that I need to do in my life, I am not ready to die yet!"

Jess shot him with Arran speaking. "Well done, that was a really good shot, Jess, I am glad that you ignored his plea to stay alive before he shot us, I would rather be deafened than dead, there will be more people here in a minute with the gunshot noises, please look around to see if anybody is tied up!"

Jess looked around her. "Thank you, no, I can't see anybody tied up, but there is a man locked up in a cage wearing handcuffs with a gag on his mouth that smells a little bit sweaty, Arran!"

Arran sounded upset. "Watch your back, Jess, because we have got company, someone has just walked in, and I can hear their footsteps walking towards us, it is making me feel frightened!"

Back in Scarborough, Ethan and Jim were planning their entry into the house, with Ethan suggesting. "I have brought the geek flower to knock her out, then we can enter when she has fallen asleep, I think that is the best plan, Jim, what do you think?"

Jim agreed. "I think that is the best plan that we are going to have at this moment in time, I will put the geek flower through the letterbox if you like Ethan!"

Ethan nodded. "Okay, yes please, Jim!"

Jim smiled. "We need to leave it a while so that she is knocked out properly in case she was not near the door, Ethan, and while we are waiting, what sort of flower uses electricity?"

Ethan looked puzzled. "I don't know what the answer is, and we have left it a good half an hour, let's break in and see if we can find Neil before she wakes up, Jim!"

Jim agreed, giving the answer. "The answer is a power plant, you distract any people walking near the house, Ethan, while I break in and find out if Neil is in there!"

Ethan laughed. "I like that joke, and please do it as silently as possible, Jim, to attract the least attention to us!"

Jim nodded yes. "I will do Ethan, I could only think of talking through the letterbox, she is lying on the floor in the lounge, I will have a look around while you stand guard!"

Jim's phone rang with Ethan on the caller identification. "Jim, it is me Ethan, you need to hide because there is a man about to enter inside of the front door at any second!"

Jim sounded panicked. "Oh, I am panicking now that you have just told me that, I will hide under the bed!"

Back in Blackpool, Arran walloped the man around the back of his head, knocking him out, then whispered to Ethan on the phone, sounding a little bit stressed. "Me and Jess need your help because we may have found John, and we are frightened for our lives!"

Chapter Six

Lifeless

Ethan sounded a little stressed. "I feel that my time is torn between you and Jim, I will drive over to you as soon as we have found out if Neil is here in Scarborough!"

Arran sounded worried. "Okay, please hurry, Ethan, me and Jess will try not to get shot any more than I already am, or I will be in so much pain, and I will struggle to walk!"

Jess looked sad. "Look, he looks lifelessly poorly in the cage, Arran; I feel sad for him!"

Arran spoke fast. "Me and Jess will find the key and get you out, what is your name?"

The man looked energy-less. "My name is John, I have been stuck in here a while that is why I smell a little bit sweaty, I was kidnapped by the staff that work here in this hotel ready for me to enter into the game, so they said!"

Jess smiled. "My name is Jess, and this is Arran, we are here to take you away from this terrible, life-threatening situation if we get out of here alive, John!"

John looked exhausted. "Thank you for picking the lock with your hair clip Jess, I felt so weak, claustrophobic and trapped, I am so glad that you are here to save me, and are they my shoes that you are wearing, Arran?"

Arran nodded yes. "Yes, they are your shoes, John, now that I have found you the spell, you may release them from my feet, but I would still need another pair of shoes if you are having your bullet-holed shoes back, John!"

Jess suggested. "You can wear the shoes from that dead man that I have shot, Arran!"

Arran looked in agony. "Yes, I will put them on my feet now that I can remove John's shoes, if I can put them on with the pain, Jess, we need to go before we all end up in the game!"

Jess sounded shocked. "I can't believe that me and Arran have finally found you John, and it looks like someone is playing video games, if you had the choice to be in the game would both of you lovely gentlemen want to join me with it saying enter players on the screen?"

John shook his head no. "I don't think so, I just need to be left alone and travel back to Wakefield!"

Arran smiled. "Yes, you have been through enough, John!"

Jess looked between Arran and John. "It looks like a fun thing to do; I wonder how we can all enter into the game, please come with us, John!"

John just shook his head in disgust. "I may as well talk to myself!"

Arran pointed. "Have you noticed that it has got thousands watching and playing it, with people giving ideas and suggestions on what should happen inside with the game, with the different characters having millions of public comments with different messages underneath the game on the screen?"

John sounded thirsty. "It sounds like a popular game, I suppose we could try this button on the computer keyboard Jess, before we do try it, I really need a drink because the people that put me into this cage did not feed me much, Arran!"

Arran offered. "Me and Jess will get you a drink and help you up John, I just wish that my left foot was not in so much pain, John, from being shot!"

John looked at his shoe. "I know it is odd having a bullet hole in my shoe, now that I have had a drink, let's press the button to see if we can go into the game, Arran and Jess!"

Jess sounded serious. "We need to stop being silly John and Arran because we will never enter into the game, let's get out of this room before he comes around from me walloping him around the head not long since, then we have to set off to Scarborough to meet Jim and Ethan!"

John asked. "I will phone my friend Ethan to tell him that I am safe, and we are on our way to Scarborough, can I please borrow your phone, Jess or Arran?"

Arran suggested. "It is a short walk over the road to the train station, John, please walk with me and Jess while you are on the phone to Ethan!"

Jess looked at the train information boards for Scarborough. "Now that we are at Blackpool train station, we need to get on the correct train, please look at what platform we need, John and Arran, and do you know what the mother train said to her little train to make him eat?"

John walked towards Jess first. "I don't know the answer, it looks like we need to get on at platform one, Jess!"

Jess sounded a little more relieved. "Now that we are on the train, we can chill out until we get there, do you gentlemen want a drink and a bacon and egg sandwich fetching and the answer is, here comes the choo choo-train!"

Arran sounded puzzled. "That is a good joke, Jess, and I just can't stop wondering why it said to enter into the game that was a bit random, what do you think, Jess and John, and yes, please?"

Jess smiled. "Someone must be playing the game, maybe Arran, and I also think that is the simplest explanation!"

Arran grinned back. "Thank you for your opinion, Jess!"

John looked out of the window in deep thought. "How do you find a missing train?"

Jess looked up. "What is the answer, John?"

Arran shrugged his shoulders. "I don't know, I have got no idea, the same as Jess?"

John answered, "You need to hire an expert to follow the tracks."

Jess laughed. "You have got some good jokes, John!"

Hours ticked by.

Arran announced. "We have arrived in Scarborough, Jess and John."

The conductor announced that they had to stay on the train for a while because there was an incident, but they could get off shortly.

Chapter Seven

Ouch

Back in the house in Scarborough, the man was shouting out the name Jenny. "What is wrong with you Jenny, you need to get up, or do I need to phone an ambulance for you and who is upstairs because I have just heard the floorboard creak and what is this flower on the floor?"

Jim rang Ethan in a panic. "I am speaking in a low tone of voice because he heard me upstairs trying to crawl under the bed with the floorboards creaking, it is okay because I have just had an idea, I will climb down the drainpipe to get out!"

Ethan sounded panicked. "I will put the phone down Jim so that you can put your phone in your pocket, but it looks like it is too late because we need an ambulance instead because the drainpipe has fallen off and you are hovering over the garden causing a scene with a few onlookers laughing at you, your trousers are falling down your legs showing your sky-blue underpants with yellow spots on them!"

Jim screamed. "Please catch me, Ethan, while I jump!"

Ethan laughed. "It is too late, Jim, sorry because you have landed in a bush and the man is standing at the side of the bush with a knife in his hand looking at you with an angry-looking red face!"

The man sounded angry. "What were you doing in our house? I do not like trespassers, and I am warning you, if you give me the answer that I do not like, I cannot guarantee a nice reaction!"

Jim explained. "My name is Jim, please give me a break, that bush hurt my bottom so much that I bet my underpants are left full of holes, and it isn't even Sunday, I was looking for Neil, who is missing!"

The man laughed. "Okay, what do you get if you get kicked by a dinosaur on the bottom?"

Jim whimpered back. "I don't know."

The man shouted. "A mega sorer ass if you don't go now before I change my mind or do something that I will regret, and did you put this strange flower in our house?"

Jim sounded upset. "Yes, it is a special flower that I must have dropped, I will take it back with me and then try to crawl away to Ethan, thank you for sparing my life!"

He sounded serious. "I will just say that you are lucky that I didn't hurt you any more than you are already injured!"

Jim walked away and rang Ethan. "I am very saw, and I have got the yellow Geek flower in my pocket, but I have got no clue what to do from now on Ethan, what do you suggest that we do now?"

Ethan sounded reassured. "Don't worry, Jim, let's go and meet up with John, Arran and Jess when they get here in Scarborough to discuss other ways to find Neil!"

Hours ticked by.

Ethan asked the lady at the train station desk. "It looks like John, Jess and Arran's train from Scarborough is here, this is correct, isn't it?"

The lady nodded yes. "It arrived a while ago, yes!"

Ethan sounded happy. "Good, we can now all search for Neil!"

Jim looked inside of the train windows because John, Jess and Arran had arrived with Ethan speaking. "I can't wait to welcome John especially!"

Jim sounded positive. "You will be happy to see John because you thought that you had lost him forever, Ethan!"

Ethan sounded a little emotional. "I know you are making me feel a little bit tearfully happy to see John again, Jim!"

Jess stepped off the train first. "Hello, I hope that Scarborough has got less commotion going on with nobody trying to kill us because it was scary in Blackpool!"

Arran left the train next. "I am glad that the commotion is sorted out so that we can get off, look, that strange video game that we noticed earlier in the Savoy hotel kitchen is over there!"

John left last. "Let's go and have a look at the game!"

Jim insisted. "We have not got time to play games because we need to find Neil, and also why do you think cats are good at video games?"

Ethan looked at everyone. "I would like to know the answer, I am just thinking out loud, I know this is silly, but I am sure that I just heard Neil's voice shouting at me from the game!"

Jim answered. "Because they have got nine lives."

John laughed. "Very funny, there is no chance that Neil will be in the game, you must be hearing voices, Ethan!"

Chapter Eight

Paper

Jess smiled. "We could investigate the game, is anybody else in favour of coming with me?"

It fell silent for a split second, with Ethan bursting with speech. "I would really like to go into the game to find out if my friend Neil is in there!"

John replied softly. "Okay, let's take a vote, everyone but Ethan, please put your hands up if you want to take the risk into the unknown!"

Jim sounded shocked. "It looks like we are all going into the game with all of our hands up voting, yes!"

Arran put his hands near to the buttons. "I have not got a clue how we enter into the game because it isn't pulling us in, I am more than sure that Neil will not be in there, anyway!"

Just as they were about to walk away from the game, Jess picked up a piece of paper that flew out of the game screen. "Look, this says if you put your fingerprint on the paper, you can join me, but the main mystery is that it doesn't say who it is from!"

Ethan calmly answered. "I will touch the paper first if you all follow me in!"

John nodded up and down with his head. "Yes, we will follow you in, but the last person needs to try to keep hold of the paper instead of letting it go to others!"

Jess put her hand up for attention. "I will touch the paper last and make sure that I keep a tight hold of it!"

Ethan vanished into the game, with Jim, Arran, John, and Jess following.

Jim looked a little bit puzzled. "It is a little bit strange that we all ended up with a piece of paper flying out of the game at us each, and I am just thinking about the last time that I played a game for ten hours, I got automatically put onto a website that said that it was a site for saw eyes!"

John laughed, looking around and then mentioned. "That's funny Jim, I really can't work this place out, because it is strange with it being full of trees with the United Kingdom's North Yorkshire Scarborough beach in the background and the Diving Belle statue in the distance further away, and do you know what the tree wore to the pool party?"

Ethan replied in a puzzled tone. "I don't know what the tree wore, and can I explain that I thought that it was where I thought Neil was, but I never imagined him inside of a game!"

John looked. "The tree wore his swimming trunks to go swimming."

Jim mentioned. "I like that and look at all of the pretty flowers, they are trying to reach their petals out to us by crawling over to us, I have never seen a flower move like a human before, and they thistle in the wind while they travel!"

Jess looked at the petals. "I like the way that you changed the word to thistle instead of whistle, maybe we need to touch the petals to see if we can get to Neil and do you know the flower that went on a date with another flower, they made a budding romance!"

John smiled. "That is so cool, and we have got nothing to lose now that we are here!"

Arran looked up. "People are coming towards us with large blades of grass in their hands, and do you know what a short cow is called in tall grass?"

John laughed. "What is the answer, and at least they can't hurt us with grass!"

Arran announced the answer. "The cow was udderly tickled."

Jess shrieked. "They can still tickle us or scrape our skin, and I do like your joke, Arran!"

Ethan replied in a low tone. "I have got a bit of useless information, did you know that cow in French means vache, and we will find out in a second if they hurt us!"

Jim had a scary thought. "I wonder what they will do to us!"

One of the men from the game handed everyone a large blade of grass and a piece of paper. "You need to put your blade of grass on the floor in front of you and walk on it without falling over!"

Chapter Nine

Diving Belle

John asked the man. "What do we do with the paper?"

Reply. "You will find out in time."

The man walked away.

Jess stood on the grass first. "I don't know what will happen if I fall, and do you know what you get if you cross a snowman with a vampire?"

Arran sounded puzzled. "I wish that I knew the answer and we may meet Neil in part of the game if we fall off, I hope!"

Jess answered. "Frostbite."

Jim looked at his grass. "That is a good joke, I will now walk on the pleasantly sweet but sharp-scented freshly cut grass, I like the smell as I walk, this is so easy!"

Ethan took his turn. "This grass is a little bit slippery to walk on, I hope that I don't fall over and hurt myself!"

John started to walk on the grass, falling over. "I feel like my voice is echoing!"

Jim cried out. "Your voice is echoing as you fall, with us hearing a splash from you!"

John's voice echoed back. "I am swimming next to the diving Belle statue floating around in the cold salty Scarborough Sea trying not to drink it with it splashing into my face, this reminds me, why are spiders good swimmers?"

Jess replied in a puzzled tone. "I don't know, and that is strange because the Diving Belle statue is normally stood proudly at the end of Scarborough Pier!"

John echoed back. "Because they have got webbed feet and Diving Belle is swimming beside me, I think that there is something wrong here!"

Arran asked. "I don't know how you can tell jokes when you are in danger, but I like it, is there anything to grab hold of to stop you from drowning?"

John echoed back. "Yes, Blackpool Tower is on the dry land a body length away from me, but the tide is stopping me from getting to it, with the waves being so high and fierce, splashing over my head and blurring my vision!"

Ethan replied in a passionate tone of voice. "I will fall off my blade of grass and join you, John!"

John shouted back. "No, please don't, because it is exhausting trying to keep my head above the waves to stay alive and breathe!"

Jim howled. "John has warned you, Ethan, we don't want to lose you as well!"

Ethan replied. "I know that it is dangerous, but I can't lose John as well as Neil!"

Jess reached out to grab Ethan's hand before he fell. "I just missed your hand, Ethan, with them sliding past each other, I am sorry about that!"

Ethan echoed back. "You may as well join us now that me and John are down here and explore what is here if we ever get out of this choppy, unsettled water in one piece alive!"

Jim, Arran, and Jess immediately joined Ethan and John with Diving Belle helping everybody onto Blackpool Tower speaking. "I have had a bit of excitement and flexibility for a change; I get fed up with people just passing me by with most people just staring at me, talking among themselves!"

Jess replied in a surprised tone. "I don't normally talk to statues, but I am glad that you enjoyed helping us, thank you!"

Ethan waved. "See you again soon Diving Belle, I could have sworn that I just heard Neil's voice again in between what it sounds like the Pleasure Beach with all of the noise from the music near to all of the rides and how does NASA plan a party?"

John sounded sad. "I sadly don't know, and I really don't think that Neil is here or listening in!"

Ethan gave the answer. "They planet."

Jim laughed. "I like that, have you thought that Neil may be watching us and organising the game, making us behave like puppets on a string?"

Jess announced. "We will find out as the adventure goes on further, won't we!"

John announced. "Yes, because someone is supplying the items for us to use, it certainly doesn't feel like we are in a game, it feels more like a nightmare!"

Chapter Ten

Juggling

Arran sounded a little puzzled. "It is strange because Blackpool Tower is on one side of this island and Blackpool Pleasure Beach is on the other side of the island, with fruit hanging from trees in between the two!"

Jess looked at her piece of paper from the game. "It says on this piece of paper that we have got to juggle fruit from the trees above us and not drop it for a minute each!"

Arran smiled. "Juggling seems fun, but I just don't have the balls to do it!"

John looked up at the fruit. "That sounds like a difficult thing to do, and I think that we are going to struggle to get the fruit off the trees with them being so high up!"

Jim stared at the fruit in deep thought. "It is not a fig deal because we could share the fruit by passing the same fruit to each other!"

Ethan grabbed fruit from the tree. "I like the fig comment instead of big, who is going to time me?"

Arran looked puzzled. "The paper in my hand has got a counter on it working automatically, so as soon as you start juggling, it will tick down on its own, and the other day the street clock spoke to the high clock saying. Hi there!"

Ethan started juggling. "We are a cheerful bunch even though we are in a dangerous, unpredictable, scary situation, look I have not dropped any of my fruit, I am obviously a pro!"

Jess suggested. "I will go next, oh, no, I have just dropped my apple, my feet are hovering in the air with no way down, it is frightening with me having no control!"

Arran tearfully shouted back. "Don't worry, Jess, we will try to get you back down!"

John sounded a bit down. "There is no chance of us reaching Jess, I think that we all need to drop some fruit, and then we can join Jess in the air!"

Arran juggled some fruit with Ethan, John and Jim doing the same, dropping it.

Jim looked around him. "We have landed in the Haunted Mansion in Blackpool, and it says above that we need to say the secret password to avoid the wolves, the other day I walked into a bar and asked for the WI-FI password."

The bartender mentioned to me. "You need to buy a drink first."

Jim. "Okay, I will have a Coke."

Bartender. "Is Pepsi, okay?"

Jim. "Sure, how much is that?"

Bartender. "£3."

Jim. "There you go, so what's the Wi-Fi password?"

Bartender. "You need to buy a drink first, no spaces, all lowercase."

Jess laughed, looking thankful, cuddling everyone in the air. "I am glad that you followed me!"

Ethan looked puzzled in the face. "How do we know what the secret password is, and we are going back down heading for the wolves' mouths?"

Arran was in deep thought. "We need to find the password now before we are eaten by wolves!"

John started to shout out random words. "Open, though, Blackpool, Diving Belle, I give up, has anybody got any better ideas?"

Jim sounded upset. "It could be literally anything, the password!"

Jess bellowed in tears. "We don't know the password, so you are going to have to set your wolves on us!"

Arran started to cry with Jess. "I am sad that we have to say goodbye to each other, it was nice knowing you all!"

Suddenly the doors opened up, with it saying enter above.

Ethan looked shocked, with a dropped jaw. "It must be something that you said that saved us, Arran!"

John looked up at the ceiling. "I am glad that we are away from the wolves, I can remember coming in here not long since, I love Blackpool Pleasure Beach!"

Jim looked down at his feet. "I am more than sure that the floor is moving because I feel unsteady on my feet!"

Jess stood with her feet apart, trying not to fall. "Yes, the floor is moving, but it is better than being eaten by wolves!"

Chapter Eleven

Neil

Arran walked along slowly. "We are walking along one side of the room; it is like the room is pulling us to one side, and do you know what happened to the wolf that swallowed a clock?"

Ethan sounded puzzled. "I don't know, but I think that some magnets are pushing us about or some kind of invisible force!"

Arran answered. "He got ticks."

John smiled. "I enjoyed your joke; look, it says that we need to enter through this door with no key!"

Jess asked. "Can anybody pick locks because it is someone else's turn?"

Jim pushed the door. "The door is open, look, there is a bouncy castle in the middle of the room with someone bouncing on it!"

Ethan was shocked. "Is that really you, Neil?"

Neil cried. "Yes, it is me, where have you all come from? I got trapped inside of this game because I was too nosy by touching the paper that I should have never touched, the same as the rest of you?"

Jim looked happy. "We were nosy as well, I am glad that you are finally found, we just need to get out of this game now!"

Jess, Jim, John, Ethan, and Arran joined Neil on the bouncy castle.

Jess spoke. "I think that I have got a phobia of bouncy castles because they always make me jump!"

John laughed. "Very funny."

There was a handwritten note on the bouncy castle wall saying. Bounce as high as you can with them bouncing high, with Jim vanishing through the floor of the castle.

Jess shrieked. "Here we go again!"

Neil answered. "It has been like this since I have been here, but I seem to have been stuck here for a while until now!"

Arran demanded. "Everyone bounce high, then we can hopefully bounce down to Jim!"

Ethan mentioned. "We are in a bed of tall grass that we can get lost in with it wrapping around our bodies!"

John suggested. "So, this is where they got the tall blades of grass from!"

Jim sounded happy. "Yes, I am just glad that you have joined me!"

Arran sounded fed up. "This game is very unpredictable; people will be laughing at us on the television screen on the outside of this game!"

Jess read her piece of paper. "It says that we have to build a shelter with the grass and then set our shelter on fire!"

They started to build their shelter, then struggled to set it on fire with having no matches to make an inferno.

Neil looked at his shelter burn with the flames saying. "Save Blackpool Tower from being swallowed up by the sea!"

Ethan sounded concerned. "How can we stop the water from covering Blackpool Tower?"

Arran laughed. "How has Blackpool Tower just appeared in front of us?"

Jim suggested. "Start scooping the water away from it with your hands!"

John scooped the most water. "My arm is aching now!"

Neil screamed. "We have all ended up inside of the lion enclosure, now I think that we are all dead!"

Ethan started shaking erratically with fear. "They are coming towards us; someone give me an idea of what to do now?"

Jess looked upset. "Panic, but don't show that we are panicking, we must be in Blackpool Zoo!"

Arran looked frightened. "A lion looks like it is about to attack me!"

Neil looked in his pocket. "I have got a piece of grass in my pocket from earlier; I will tickle the lion to see if that helps!"

John looked frightened, pulling strange faces. "It looks like they are eyeing me up for their dinner as well!"

Jim watched Neil tickling the lion with it working. "That's one lion distracted, has anybody else got more grass?"

Chapter Twelve

Ice

Ethan looked distressed. "We need to get out of here, it is scary, and do you know what the lion said when he was about to go hunting?"

Jess looked at everyone. "This is not the right time for jokes, but please give me the answer!"

Ethan replied. "I was only trying to lighten the mood, let's pray!"

Arran gave a grin. "At least we are a little bit more cheered up now, goodbye everyone, I think that this is our last day alive because the lion is about to attack me!"

Neil looked up. "The lions have turned into house cats, what kind of game is this?"

Arran looked at his paper. "It says that the only way to end the game is to hit the target with the darts!"

Jim looked puzzled. "I want to know where we can get these darts from?"

John stared at the enclosure that they were in, with it all changing around them into the Blackpool Pleasure Beach ice skating rink. "It feels cold in here with the ice at the side of the rink, I always wanted to get into ice skating, but when it comes to it, I always get cold feet!"

Ethan looked at the ice. "Very funny, I can see a target in the middle of the ice rink floor with nobody on it!"

Jess looked at the ice cream store. "I wonder if ice cream would work as darts for a target?"

Neil walked over to the ice cream lady. "Could we please buy all of the ice cream in tubs that you have got available?"

Arran walked over to Neil. "I will help you to carry all of the ice creams!"

Jim walked over to help to carry the ice cream as well. "Do you know why ice cream is always at a party, and I hope that this works so that we can get out of this game."

Arran shook his head no. "I don't know?"

Jim answered. "Because he is always the coolest there!"

Ethan threw an ice cream tub at the target first. "I like that the strawberry ice cream smells so sweet and fresh, come on, Neil, Jess, Ethan, John and Arran, you need to do this as well if we have got any chance of getting out of this game!"

Ice cream covered the floor, with it spilling out of the tubs, with nobody winning because it was just one big slippery mess with John speaking. "We will have to find another target because it has got no obvious winner, and it has just made me really want some ice cream, my favourite flavour by far is chocolate!"

Jess sounded happy. "At least we can enjoy the ice cream that is left over!"

Arran agreed. "True, the room is changing into large water fountains around us as we have just finished eating our ice cream, maybe there will be some kind of target that we can hit here!"

Jim smiled. "Maybe we could use ourselves as a target!"

Neil's face dropped like a sack of potatoes. "That means that we will get very wet, but I suppose that we will have to just go with the flow because we have got no choice in the matter!"

Jim looked hopeful. "It is a good idea because there is nothing else around for us to use, I wonder water we are doing later!"

Jess put her hands up. "I like the way that you put water instead of what, I will volunteer to get wet first!"

Ethan interrupted. "We all need to go into the centre target together, so that we can hopefully travel back together out of the game!"

John shared his thoughts. "Yes, you are correct, Ethan, then we can hopefully get out of this game sooner rather than later!"

Chapter Thirteen

Penguins

Ethan looked up at the water flying over their heads, with it dancing around with loud pop music playing. "Look, that round target is just like a dartboard in the middle of the water fountain, and do you know what Father Christmas waters his vegetables with?"

Neil answered. "I don't know the answer!"

Ethan answered. "His hose, hose, hose!"

Jess laughed. "I like that, and I love Christmas!"

Jess led the way, with John, Ethan, Arran, Neil, and Jim following.

Jim slipped, knocking everybody over. "It looks like we are out of luck, the exit to the game is over, and we are staying a little bit longer wet through and cold!"

Neil pointed out. "Look, penguins are walking towards us, we must be in the Sea Life Centre in Scarborough or Blackpool maybe, and do you know why we don't see penguins in Britain apart from in the zoo?"

Arran asked. "Why don't we have penguins in Britain?"

Neil answered. "Because they don't like whales and Wales as a country!"

John laughed. "You are funny, Neil, with you saying the animal whales!"

Jess pointed out. "Look at that penguin, it has got a target on it's stomach what can we use that is soft for the target?"

Ethan found a feather on the floor. "I found a feather the other day and did a poll asking if people preferred feathers or synthetic inside of their pillows, but synthetic didn't win because there were too many downvotes, and I suggest that we could take turns with this feather hoping that we all hit the middle target and leave the game!"

Arran laughed. "That's cool!"

Neil and John threw the feather first, with them hitting the target on the penguin's stomach, with them leaving the game immediately.

Arran moaned. "The feather has broken in half, so we can't carry on with the game to release us all!"

Outside of the game at Scarborough train station, Neil looked shell-shocked to be out of the game. "I can't believe that we are out of the game, I hope that Arran, Jess, Ethan and Jim follow us out of the game!"

John looked at Neil with a hopeful expression. "Me too, I really thought that they would have appeared by now, we will have to get comfy and wait for them to appear, I tried to apply for a job as a train conductor not long ago, but they said that I didn't have enough training!"

Neil agreed, laughing. "Yes, let's sit at the side of the game and relax!"

<u>Back in the game,</u> Jim looked sad. "This is getting really silly!"

Jess scowled back in anger. "Please just let us go now, this is totally ridiculous!"

Arran spoke calmly. "There is no point in getting angry, Jess, because it will not change anything!"

Jess replied. "I can't help it, sorry!"

Ethan smirked. "It should be me who is angry because I am separated from my friends Neil and John again, I am finding it hard to hold back my tears!"

Jim announced. "I am sorry to interrupt your conversation, but look at my paper, it says that we need to swim up and down in the Alpamare Water

Park in Scarborough four times in front of us doing full lengths, then we need to get the ball into the net so that we can leave the game!"

Jess miserably answered. "We will be even colder than we already are doing that, but if it gets us out of here, I will do it!"

Ethan looked tired. "Do you know what the ocean said to the beach?"

Jim replied. "I don't know?"

Ethan answered. "Nothing, he just waved!"

Jim laughed.

Arran, Jess, Ethan, and Jim jumped into the swimming pool, complaining about how cold it was, fully clothed.

Jim blurted out. "I bet Neil and John are drying off now, they are so jammy!"

Ethan shivered with his teeth chattering. "Yes, they are lucky!"

Arran replied. "I have made it to the end, and my ball is going in the net!"

Chapter Fourteen

Us three

Back outside of the game, John welcomed Arran. "You are even wetter than you were before, what have you been doing?"

Arran replied with chattering teeth from shaking. "Swimming four lengths and throwing a ball into a net!"

Neil spoke in a concerned tone. "That is why you are so cold; I will find something to warm you up!"

A lady walking past handed Arran a towel as she walked along. "You need this more than I do, you look absolutely freezing!"

Arran thanked the lady as she walked away. "You will hopefully get rewarded for kindness one day, thank you again!"

John smiled. "There are some kind people about, at least you are out of that terrible game with us now!"

Back in the game, Jess, Ethan, and Jim missed the net.

Ethan spoke. "At least Arran has made it out of the game, it is just us three now left to get out!"

Jess looked in front of her, shivering. "Look on the notice board that has appeared, it says that we need to stop shivering for a minute if we want to leave the game!"

Ethan attempted to lighten the mood. "This reminds me, my friends parrot kept swearing, *so* he threatened to put the parrot into the freezer if he didn't stop swearing, the parrot was warned again with him not stopping swearing and he then put the parrot into the freezer for a few minutes and asked it if it would stop swearing, the parrot replied with, I will stop swearing but what the heck did the turkeys do to be put in there?"

Jess laughed. "That's funny."

Three towels appeared from the sky, and the Alpamare swimming pool vanished, with a snowstorm appearing in front of them.

Ethan advised Jim and Jess. "We need to wrap ourselves in the towels and grit our teeth and try not to shiver so that we can all leave this game!"

Jess pointed out the stopwatch on the notice board, with it counting down from three, two, one, then a minute started ticking away.

Jim, Ethan, and Jess gritted their teeth, trying to stop shivering with their towels wrapped around them as tightly as they could get them.

A minute was up, and Jim vanished.

Jess spoke. "It looks like me and you, Ethan didn't stay still enough to leave the game; this is making me feel even angrier!"

<u>**Outside of the game, Jim was**</u>
transported to John, Neil and Arran, and
they welcomed Jim with open arms.

Jim spoke. "We need to find the
people who have invented this game and
put them in it!"

John replied. "I totally agree with
you, sit and relax with us!"

<u>Back in the game, Jess and Ethan</u> looked wet, cold, and fed up.

Ethan looked up. "It is saying on the notice board that we have got to pick these translation books up and find the word circle in Spanish, and I am just thinking, do you know what the triangle said to the circle?"

Jess had a lightbulb moment. "I have got no idea!"

Ethan answered. "You're pointless!"

Jess giggled. "I have started looking, if we both find a circle together, we should hopefully leave the game together!"

Ethan shouted out. "Circulo is the answer!"

Ethan immediately disappeared.

<u>Back outside of the game, Jim, John, Neil, and Arran welcomed Ethan.</u>

Arran spoke sadly. "I feel really sad for Jess being left in the game alone, I would hate that!"

Neil reassured Arran. "Jess can get out; don't worry, she is stronger than you think!"

<u>**Back in the game, Jess was crying.**</u>
"I am so frightened of what future things I have got to do to get out of here!"

On the notice board, it said to hop for a minute without falling over.

As the minute started to pass by, Jess hopped, switching feet. "I think that I have finally made it out of this traumatic game!"

Chapter Fifteen

Train

Back outside of the game, Jess joined Jim, John, Neil, Arran, and Ethan. "I can't help but cry to be back with you all, let's cuddle for a second, it will feel more real that I am out and with you all!"

Jim replied, wiping a tear away. "I am shocked that we all got out alive!"

Neil replied. "Come on, we really do need to find out who has done this to us!"

John sounded a little stressed. "Where do we start?"

Arran mentioned. "The person who shot me earlier was talking about controlling the game, so something is going on in the Savoy Hotel, so we really do need to go back to the Blackpool hotel where I got shot in my left foot in my opinion, I think!"

Ethan suggested. "I am just thinking that we need to get the train to Witch Wakefield to see if she can cast a spell so that the hotel staff have got no choice but to enter into the game!"

Jim smiled. "With the information that you have just said, I am just thinking that we need to go to Wakefield and get a spell on a utensil for the kitchen that they need to use or pour a potion straight onto the staff working there!"

John sounded positive. "That is settled then, we need a train to Wakefield in West Yorkshire!"

Arran pointed. "Look, let's jump on the Wakefield train that is just there!"

They boarded the train with Jim speaking. "At least we are on our way to Witch Wakefield."

Hours ticked by.

Ethan replied. "At least we have arrived in Wakefield, we just need to get the train to her house in Crofton and hope that she is in!"

Jess suggested. "Now that we are nearly there, let's get off the bus and walk the rest of the way to <u>Witch Wakefield's house!</u>"

Ethan replied. "Now that we are here, I will knock at the door!"

The door opened before Ethan could knock, with Witch Wakefield standing at the door. "Come in, how can

I help you all, it is nice to see you again, Ethan!"

Ethan replied. "It is nice to see you again, your spell on the shoes worked because I have got John and Neil back, I can't thank you enough!"

Jim interrupted. "I am sorry to barge in on your conversation, but we need some kind of control spell that can be used to make people go into the game!"

Witch Wakefield replied. "This is a potion that I made the other day, you just need to throw the contents of the bag at whoever you need to control, and they will do exactly what you say for about a day!"

Jess replied. "Thank you, Witch Wakefield, for the spell, we really have got to go because we are on a mission!"

As they walked out, Neil was holding the potion. "At least we are on our way to the Savoy Hotel in Blackpool, let's just hope that we don't get shot!"

John looked scared. "I will go for a walk along the beach because they may recognise me and lock me up again, and before I go, how do you make an octopus laugh?"

Neil asked. "I don't know?"

John answered. "Give it ten tickles!"

Jess laughed. "I like that, you enjoy your walk John, see you soon!"

Ethan pulled the yellow geek flower out of his pocket. "This will knock them out for a while so that when they start to wake up, we can pour the potion on each of the staff members to control them!"

Neil walked in, smiling. "We need to hide all of the staff members away from the public immediately as soon as we have knocked them out with the sleeping smoke!"

Jim agreed. "Now that the yellow geek flower is about to knock everyone out, we need to step outside so that we don't get knocked out while Ethan sets it off with his silver key!"

Ethan put a mask on as he walked outside with hotel guests looking at him strangely as he explained. "I get bad allergies!"

Chapter Sixteen

Potion

After an hour, they walked back into the Savoy Hotel, including John, finding staff and guests lying around in various places snoring away in dreamland.

Arran looked around at everyone on the floor, recognising some of the staff from before, with them wearing their uniforms. "I will go around and squirt every staff member with you later, Ethan, as they start to wake up!"

John commented. "We can't hide them away; there are far too many people laid down!"

Jim looked around. "Yes, you are correct, John!"

Hours ticked by.

Jess looked startled. "They are starting to come around a little bit, please start to squirt them with the potion Ethan and Arran!"

Arran explained. "Me and Arran have started to share the potion out, but unfortunately for us, there isn't enough to go around!"

Neil looked disappointed. "What do we do now with there not being enough potion?"

John looked in deep thought. "We could get the manager to make the rest of the staff follow him!"

Jim looked up, startled by a lightbulb moment. "Yes, we just need to order the manager to follow us!"

Jess smiled. "Yes, and ask the manager to get his staff together so that they will follow him as Jim suggested!"

Ethan looked hopeful, yelling. "Yes, bingo, we are in complete control with me covering the staff members in the potion!"

Arran gave everyone a thumbs-up. "Now that the staff are covered in the potion, and they are groggily coming around, we will probably need to go immediately!"

Neil ordered the manager of the Savoy Hotel about. "Please tell your staff to follow you wherever you go now!"

The Savoy manager announced. "All of my staff, please follow me everywhere that I go now without stopping, no matter what happens!"

They walked into the kitchen area where they found John previously walking up to the game, with John speaking to the Savoy manager. "Please instruct your staff to enter inside of the game now by putting their hands on the paper that is on the game!"

The staff entered into the game, one at a time, with the last few about to enter with a male staff member speaking. "I don't want to enter inside of the game because I was one of the people who controlled you all when you were stuck inside of the game!"

Jim answered him. "Get into the game now or I will chop your hands off with this knife that was lying about!"

The male staff member tried to grab the knife and ended up picking up a heavy, large pan instead. "You have all had it, no more people are entering into the game, I am not sure what you have done to make people enter into the game, but it stops here!"

Jess snapped back. "Look, your colleagues are not bothered, they are entering into the game, just go in and stop carrying on!"

Other staff members pushed past the male member of staff. "Stop now and have some common sense because you will struggle to get back out of the game!"

The staff members ignored him, carrying on touching the paper and entering into the game.

The male staff member hit Arran on his left foot with Jess grabbing hold of him from the back, with Jess angrily speaking. "You need to touch that paper and get out of our sight now before we kill you because you are on your own with no help!"

Arran screamed with pain from still being in agony from the gunshot wound in his left foot earlier. "I am in so much pain, I could cry!"

Jim squinted with Arran being in so much pain. "I am making you touch that paper by grabbing hold of you, everyone help me, please, now!"

Neil forced his hands onto the paper, with him finally disappearing into the game. "We did it, they are all inside of the game, we can finally get our own back on them, let's throw everything that we can at them and let them see how it feels!"

John smiled. "I feel proud of us for doing this, let's have some fun making their lives hell as they did to us!"

Ethan searched around, finding an instruction manual. "According to this manual, we use this pen to shrink and drag items into the game for them to do!"

John mentioned. "I think that we should send some helium balloons in and ask them to suck the air in and speak so that we can laugh at their high-pitched voices!"

Chapter Seventeen

Coin

Neil nodded forward and back. "Yes, and the one with the highest pitch wins their way out of the game, I am sending the balloons in now, and when I made hot air balloons my job was up in the air because I never knew if I should quit!"

Ethan stared at the screen. "That comment was good, their voices are so comical to listen to, but I don't think that it will last long, and they look to be having too much fun!"

Jess suggested. "Let's squirt them with water on a jet with none of them winning their way out of the game using the water option with it asking us how much water we would like to send?"

Arran agreed that it was a good idea with the balloons vanishing. "We can pretend that the wettest person would win, but nobody would really win because they would be all as wet as each other!"

Jim laughed. "Their faces are so funny, and I bet they are so cold like we were!"

Ethan suggested. "I think that we should send paintballs in for them to shoot at each other and the one with the most paintballs to hit them can leave the game!"

Jess laughed. "Yes, that is a good idea because I think that they would be all as covered in paint as each other, I will use the paintball tool with the pen!"

John grinned. "They all look so fed up; I am glad that the boot is on the other foot with them getting a taste of their own medicine!"

Neil had a creepy look, with his eyes lighting up. "Let's send a large spider in and see if anybody touches it, if they touch it, they can win their way out, there is a spider here that we can enlarge when it is in the game, I am sending it in now!"

Arran sniggered. "At least none of them are touching the spider, so none of them can leave the game!"

John giggled. "We need to superglue coins to the floor and watch them try to get them from the floor!"

Ethan chuckled. "Yes, and we could promise them a way out if they can get a coin from the floor that I am organising for them now!"

Jess had a twinkling look in her eyes. "We could just leave them in the game with this challenge permanently, so that they would never leave the game!"

John joyfully replied. "Yes, now that we have completed what we set out to do, let's go home and relax, we can keep in touch with one another!"

Arran looked in pain. "I can go home and get my left foot better; I am glad that I went into the charity shop, I would definitely do it all again!"

Jim looked at Arran. "I am glad that we did this as well because it is a story to tell people in the future!"

Ethan hugged everyone. "I am really glad to have John and Neil back with me thanks to Witch Wakefield!"

Jess hugged everyone back. "It has been an adventure that I will never forget!"

They all went home and kept in touch with the Savoy hotel doors shutting to the public with it having no staff.

Six months later.

Jim rang around asking John, Arran, Ethan, and Jess if they would like to run the Savoy hotel with him, with them all agreeing.

As they moved in, a male staff member was sitting watching his friends in the kitchen, looking sad, dirty, and fed up. "So, you have come back after leaving us in the game!"

Jess got a knife from the worktop. "You left us in the game for too long, we only did the same to you and your work colleagues!"

He replied. "At least we let you out of the game eventually!"

John grabbed hold of the man, putting him into the cage and locked it.

"You can stay in there and not come out!"

Jim suggested inviting Witch Wakefield to the Savoy Hotel, so that she could make a potion that would permanently erase his memories. "What do you all think of my idea?"

Arran agreed, ringing Witch Wakefield. "Would you please make us a forget spell and bring it with you, Witch Wakefield?"

Witch Wakefield replied. "Yes, of course I will, I am a Yorkshire lady, after all, I will do this for a free break away!"

Hours ticked by.

The man started to wave the knife about every time that anybody went near. "Come any closer and I will kill you!"

They laughed at him in the cage.

Witch Wakefield arrived with the forget potion, with her throwing it onto the man. "I am one hundred percent sure that he will not hurt any of us anymore because he will have forgotten everything!"

Ethan released the man with him working for the hotel, and the rest of his ex-colleagues were stuck in the game forever, and the Savoy hotel was run like clockwork.

Jim spoke. "Just remember that there are some not-very-nice people in this world, everyone needs to be careful who they talk to!"

The End.

About the author

Anita Kirk is from Yorkshire in the United Kingdom, she works full-time and writes many book genres in her spare time with unlimited talent to write anything, she loves swimming, line dancing, holidays, music, films, writing, reading and spending time with friends and family.

All of Anita Kirk's books have got <u>funny moments</u> that may make you feel like laughing your socks off.

In a Quarter of a second and the Glowing Rings has got two magical action-packed time travel adventures inside.

Dream Changing is about a lady who can see people's dreams and can change them.
Does Flora help to save the world after visiting the opticians receiving more hassle and drama than she bargained for?

Sexy Antics is for adults to enjoy; you will never look at a magazine in the same way again.

Magical Footsteps has got a friend that has gone missing that needs finding with help from strangers, with them ending up inside of a game.

Unexpected Jewel has got different stories inside full of mythical creatures, and it is full of magic.

Sexy Shenanigans has got four stories for adults to enjoy with the last story having horror inside as well.

Christmas Sparkles has got fairies inside of this book and a fairytale cottage where they live, the fairies need help from two children and other people to get people onto the nice list to save Christmas, with so much more inside for you to enjoy.

Mel's Adventure has got a story with pictures for the younger end or anyone that needs a simple story to learn the alphabet, with a song and a few words in a different language to learn as well.

<u>The Sound of Ticking</u> is about a man who owns a shop in New York and receives a telescope for his birthday, his life is soon turned upside down with unpredictable challenging situations taking him to many places in time to solve many mysteries.

<u>Wings to Heaven</u>. This is a true story about my dad's life before,

during and after dementia and Alzheimer's.

TIME TRAVEL LIP BALM
Enjoy the adventure, the lip balm dramas inside of this book are very unpredictable and fun, it's full of jokes and lighthearted entertainment for anyone to enjoy from adults to children.

Sexy Revenge is for adults only, it's about a man that has a car accident, and his life is stolen by his best friend while he's in a coma, does Jenson kick some ass getting his own back?

Fun Dance Book One has got many dances to follow by yourself or with others, it is ideal for any age.

Spooky Scary needs garlic circles and so much more to bring people back to normal everyday life with many obstacles and drama along the way.

These books have been written so far with many more available soon.

Remember that you can follow and contact Anita Kirk with any questions or comments on Tick Tock, Facebook, Twitter, LinkedIn or you can email any comments to anitajane1@outlook.com

Please contact Anita if you would like a shop opening or anything else and she will get back to you as soon as possible with an answer.

If you have enjoyed reading Anita Kirk's books a good review would be appreciated and if you could share Anita's books on your social media, and with your family and friends she would really appreciate your help.

Thank you for your support in reading this book.
All of Anita Kirk's books are available on Amazon and some other online shops.

*__A good review would mean a lot if
you have enjoyed this book.
Thank you in advance for your good
positive review it is very much
appreciated.__*

Thank you again

PLEASE TYPE ANITA KIRK INTO AMAZON

FOR ALL AVAILABLE PUBLISHED BOOKS

OF MANY DIFFERENT GENRES.

***Erotically Spooky** is the **same** as **Spooky Scary** but it has got a little bit of raunch, and vampires attempt to take over the world with funny moments to make you laugh out loud.*

***Thank you.**

Anita Kirk, author
@AnitaKi73550337

Twitter –

Author Anita Kirk

LinkedIn-

Instagram-

Please don't forget to leave a good review if you have enjoyed reading this book and share it with others on social media or in person.

Thank you again.
You can also follow Anita Kirk on

@anitakirkauthor

tick tock.